Cinderella

p

Once upon a time, there lived a pretty little girl. Sadly, her mother died when she was young. Her father remarried, but the girl's stepmother was a mean woman with two ugly daughters. These stepsisters were so jealous of the young girl's beauty that they treated her like a servant and made her sit among the cinders in the kitchen.

They called her Cinderella, and before long everyone, even her father, had forgotten the little girl's real name.

One day, an invitation arrived from the royal palace. The king and queen were holding a ball for the prince's twenty-first birthday, and all the fine ladies of the kingdom were invited.

Cinderella's stepsisters were very excited.

"I will wear my red velvet gown!" cried the first stepsister. "And the black pearl necklace that Mother gave me."

"And I will wear my blue silk dress!" cried the other. "With a silver tiara."

"Come, Cinderella!" they called. "You must help us get ready!"

Cinderella helped her stepsisters with their silk stockings and frilly petticoats. She brushed and curled their hair and powdered their cheeks and noses. At last, she squeezed them into their beautiful ball-gowns.

But even after all this, the two ugly stepsisters weren't nearly as lovely as Cinderella was in her rags. This made them very jealous and angry, and they began to tease Cinderella.

"Too bad *you* can't come to the ball!" sneered the first stepsister.

"Yes," laughed the other one. "They'd never let a shabby creature like you near the palace!"

Cinderella said nothing, but inside, her heart was breaking. She really wanted to go to the ball. After her stepsisters left, she sat and wept.

"Dry your tears, my dear," said a gentle voice.

Cinderella was amazed. A kind old woman stood before her. In her hand was a sparkling wand.

"I am your Fairy Godmother," she told Cinderella. "And you shall go to the ball!"

"But I have nothing to wear!" cried Cinderella. "And how will I get there?"

Then the Fairy Godmother asked Cinderella to fetch her the biggest pumpkin in the garden. With a flick of her magic wand she turned it into a golden carriage and the mice in the kitchen mousetrap into fine horses. A fat rat became a coachman.

Cinderella couldn't believe her eyes.

Smiling, the Fairy Godmother waved her wand once more and suddenly Cinderella was dressed in a splendid ball-gown. On her feet were sparkling glass slippers.

"My magic will end at midnight, so you must be home before then," said the Fairy Godmother. "Good luck."

When Cinderella arrived at the ball, everyone was dazzled by her beauty. Whispers went around the ballroom as the other guests wondered who this enchanting stranger could be. Even Cinderella's own stepsisters did not recognize her.

As soon as the prince set eyes on Cinderella, he fell in love with her. "Would you give me the honor of this dance?" he asked.

"Why certainly, sir," said Cinderella. And from that moment on the prince knew he had found his true love.

Soon the clock struck midnight. "I must go!" said Cinderella, suddenly remembering her promise to her Fairy Godmother. She fled from the ballroom and ran down the palace steps. The prince ran after her, but when he got outside, she was gone. He didn't notice a grubby servant girl holding a pumpkin. A few mice and a rat scurried around her feet.

But there on the steps was one dainty glass slipper. The prince picked it up and rushed back into the palace. "Does anyone know who this slipper belongs to?" he cried.

The next day, Cinderella's stepsisters could talk of nothing but the ball, and the beautiful stranger who had danced all night with the prince. As they were talking, there was a knock at the door.

"Cinderella," called the stepmother, "quick, jump up and see who it is." Standing on the doorstep was the prince himself. Beside him was a royal footman, holding the little glass slipper on a velvet cushion.

"The lady whose foot this slipper fits is my one and only true love," said the prince. "I am visiting every house in the kingdom in search of her."

The two stepsisters began shoving each other out of the way in their rush to try on the slipper. They both squeezed and pushed as hard as they could, but their clumsy feet were far too big for the tiny glass shoe.

Then Cinderella stepped forward. "Please, Your Highness," she said shyly, "may I try?"

As her stepsisters watched in amazement, Cinderella slid her foot into the dainty slipper. It fitted as if it were made for her!

As the prince gazed into her eyes, he knew he had found the pretty girl he had danced with at the ball.

"Will you marry me?" said the prince.

"Yes, I will!" cried Cinderella.

On the day of their wedding, bells rang throughout the land, and the sun shone as people cheered. Even Cinderella's nasty stepsisters were invited to the wedding. Everyone had a wonderful day, and Cinderella and her prince lived happily ever after.